HOW PEOPLE LIVE

IN CITIES

Nancy Dickmann

BROWN BEAR BOOKS

Published by Brown Bear Books Ltd
4877 N. Circulo Bujia, Tucson, AZ 85718, USA
and
Studio G14, Regent Studios, 1 Thane Villas, London N7 7PH, UK

Text: Nancy Dickmann
Design Manager: Keith Davis
Children's Publisher: Anne O'Daly

Library of Congress Cataloging-in-Publication Data
Names: Dickmann, Nancy, author.
Title: In cities / Nancy Dickmann.
Description: Tuscon, AZ : Brown Bear Books, Ltd, [2025] | Series: Fast Track: How People Live | Includes bibliographical references and index. | Audience: Ages 5-7 | Audience: Grades K-1 | Summary: "How people live in cities all around the world"– Provided by publisher.
Identifiers: LCCN 2023052231 (print) | LCCN 2023052232 (ebook) | ISBN 9781781219706 (library binding) | ISBN 9781781219768 (paperback) | ISBN 9781781219829 (ebook)
Subjects: LCSH: Cities and towns–Juvenile literature. | Sociology, Urban–Juvenile literature.
Classification: LCC HT152 .D43 2025 (print) | LCC HT152 (ebook) | DDC 307.76–dc23/eng/20231207
LC record available at https://lccn.loc.gov/2023052231
LC ebook record available at https://lccn.loc.gov/2023052232

The photographs in this book are used by permission and through the courtesy of:
Cover: Shutterstock: Luciano Mortula - LGM. Shutterstock: AYA Images11, Fokke Baarssen 18, Willy Barton 4, Christian Bertrand 19, Cat_arch_angel 24b, Alberto Cervantes 23, Ant Clausen 12, Cultura Motion 9, davslens - davslens.com 17, Deemerwha Studio 6, EQRoy 7, Elena Istomina 1ins, 3 ins, Olga Kashubin 5, Mirko Kuzmanovic 21cr, Lazy Llama 20b, leshy985 21b, Luca9257 15, MJ Mahesh 10, marishuana 4-5bk, 12-13bk, Luciano Mortula - LGM 20t, nicor nl 1, 2-3, 20-21bk, 22-23bk, 24, Porcupen 20-21c, Preisler 14, Ram Creative 10-11bk, 18-19bk, Helen Ross 13, Sangkhom Sangkakam 16, Alex Segre 21t, Skreidzeleu 8, Vectorpocket 8-9bk, 16-17bk, VitalityVill 6-7bk, 14-15bk.
t-top, b-bottom, l-left, r-right, c-center, bk-background
All other artwork and photography © Brown Bear Books.

Brown Bear Books has made every attempt to contact the copyright holders. If you have any information about omissions please contact: licensing@brownbearbooks.co.uk.

Words in **bold** appear in the Words to Know on page 23.

Manufactured in the United States of America
CPSIA compliance information: Batch#AG/5659

Contents

Hustle and Bustle

In cities many people live in a small area.
Buildings are close together.
Cities have homes and stores.
There are offices and museums.

London, England, is about 2,000 years old. It has a mix of old and new buildings.

Cities are busy day and night.
People visit theaters and restaurants.
More than half of the world's people
live in cities.

Weather and Climate

There are cities all over the world.
Some are in hot places. Others are cold.
Some are rainy and others are dry.
Cities are usually warmer than countryside.

The air in some cities is **polluted.** Breathing it can be harmful.

Some cities have tunnels underground. People can walk from one building to another. The tunnels are cool in hot weather. They stay warm in winter.

WOW!

Minneapolis has walkways above the ground. These skyways go between buildings. They are one or two stories high.

City Homes

Cities squeeze in a lot of homes.
Some houses are built in a row.
The houses are joined together.
These are called **townhouses**.

Some cities have small houses built very close together. This city is in Brazil.

WOW!

The Ancient Romans invented apartments! They built blocks five or six stories tall. There were stores on the ground floor.

Apartment blocks are tall buildings.
Each story is divided into apartments.
People ride elevators to their floor.
They have a **balcony** instead of a yard.

Food and Drink

Cities are full of places to eat.
There are grocery stores and **delis**.
There are restaurants and cafés.
You'll find foods from around the world.

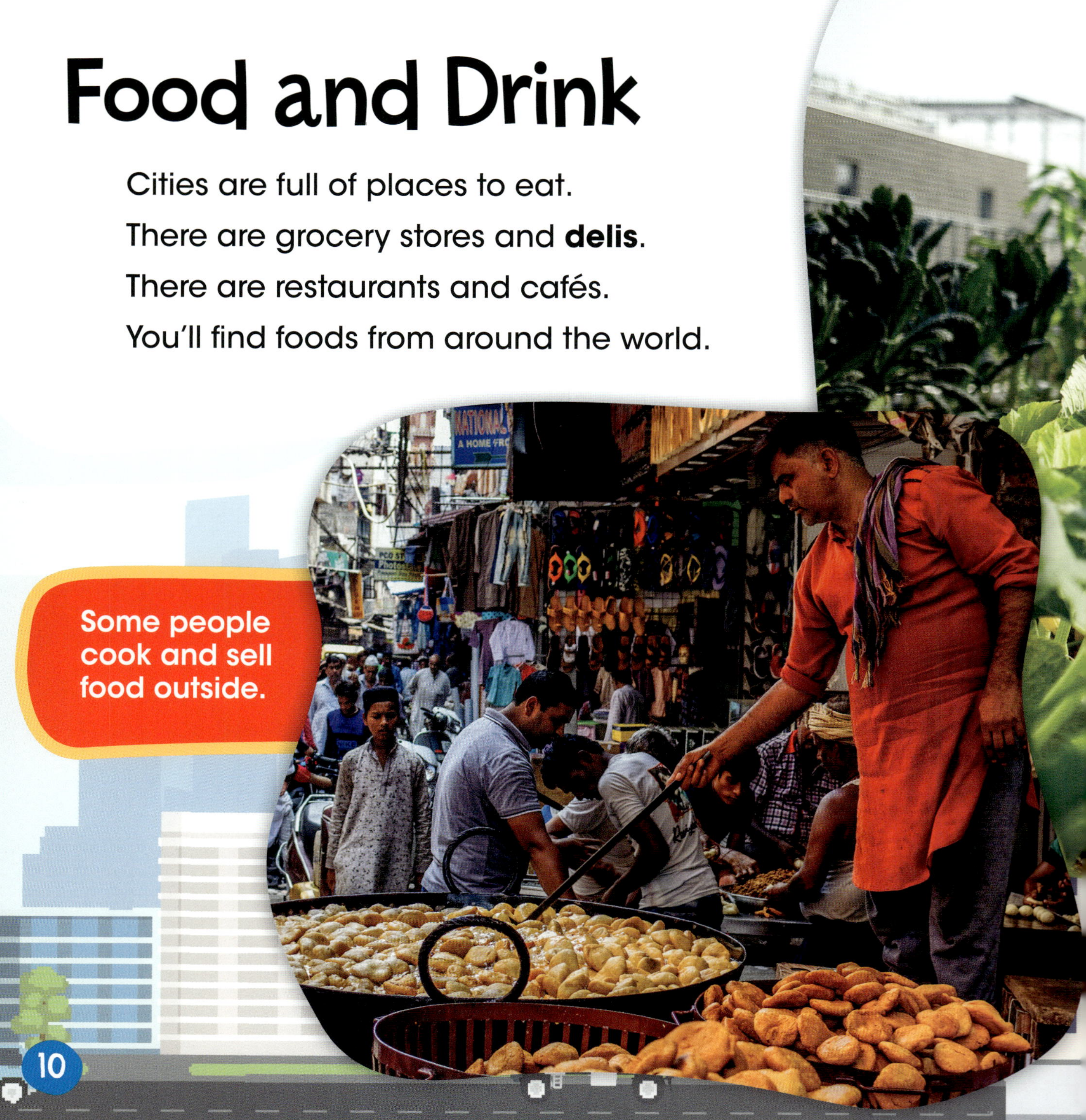

Some people cook and sell food outside.

Cities don't have fields for growing crops.
Most food arrives by truck or train.
But some people grow food.
They grow plants on the roofs of buildings.

Clothes

Many city people work in offices.
They may wear suits or dresses.
Other workers wear special clothes.
Police officers and bus drivers wear uniforms.

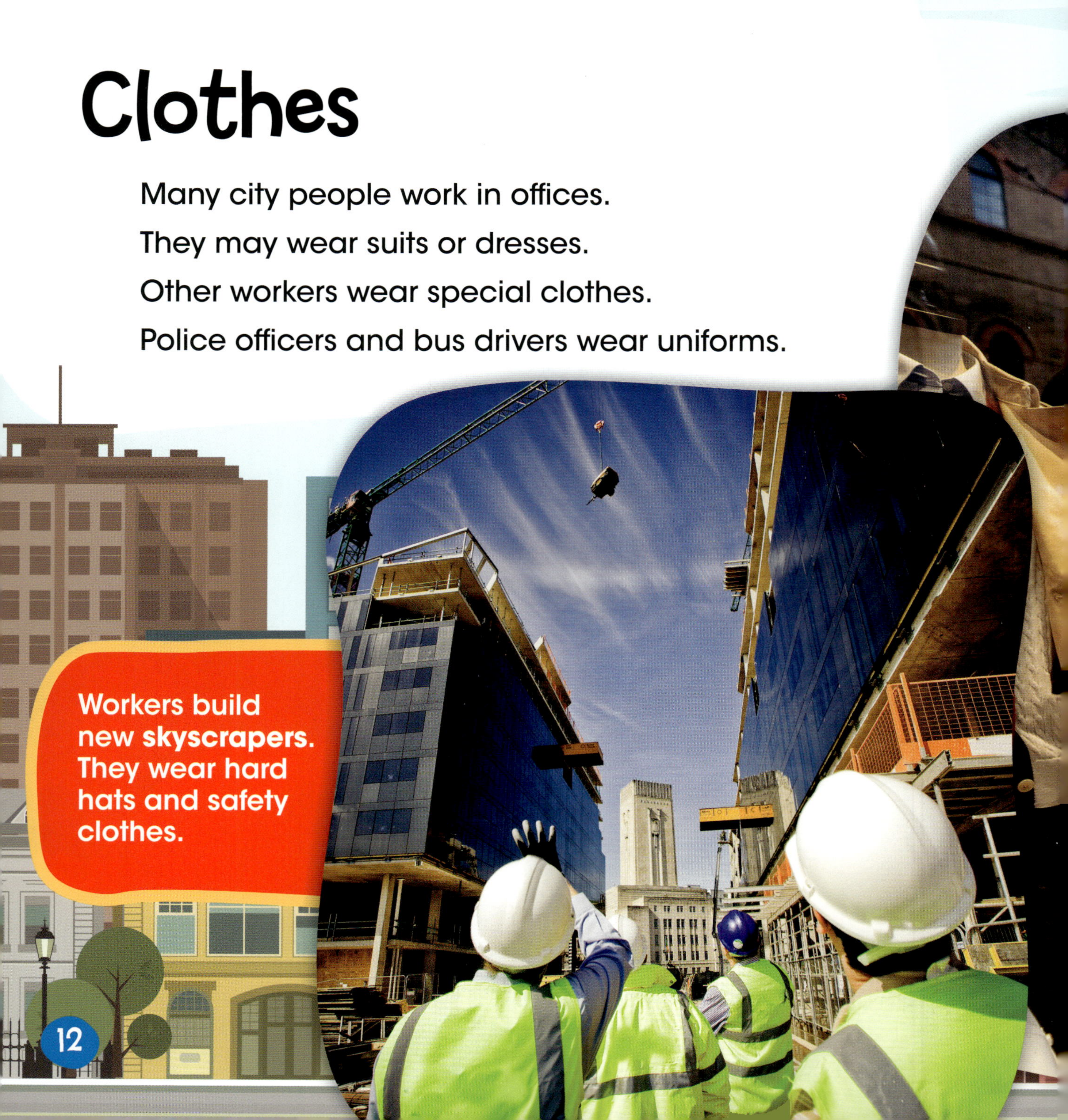

Workers build new **skyscrapers.** They wear hard hats and safety clothes.

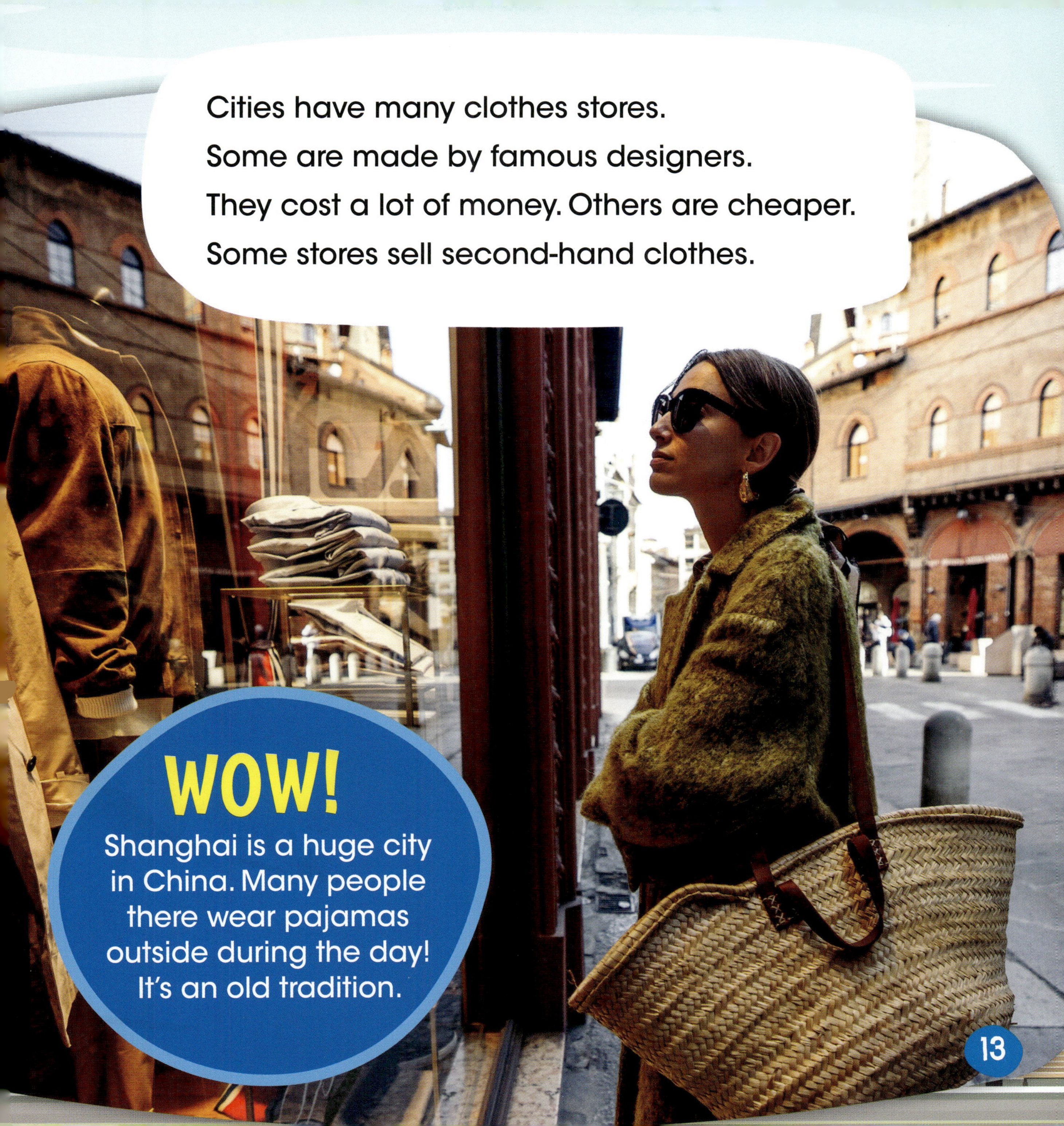

Cities have many clothes stores. Some are made by famous designers. They cost a lot of money. Others are cheaper. Some stores sell second-hand clothes.

WOW!

Shanghai is a huge city in China. Many people there wear pajamas outside during the day! It's an old tradition.

Jobs

There are all kinds of jobs in a city.
Many people work in offices.
Others help customers in stores.
There are schools and hospitals, too.

Tourists often visit big cities. Tour guides show them around.

Running a city is a big job!
Many cities have a **mayor** in charge.
Police officers keep the city safe.
Trash collectors keep it clean.
Snow plow drivers clear roads in winter.

WOW!

Cities have a lot of traffic. In Bolivia's cities, there are crossing guards. They are dressed as zebras!

Getting Around

There are lots of ways to get around.
Buses carry passengers around.
So do taxis. Many people walk or ride bikes.

Bangkok is famous for its **canals**. People get around on boats.

Many big cities have train systems.
Sometimes the trains are above ground.
In other places they are underground.
Passengers ride escalators to the platform.

WOW!

Trains can get very crowded. In Tokyo, workers push people onto trains!

Games and Sports

Cities often have large parks.
Many parks have playgrounds.
There are basketball courts.
Some are on top of buildings!

In the winter, Amsterdam's canals freeze. People ice skate on them.

Many cities are home to sports teams.
Some teams play soccer in big stadiums.
Others play baseball or rugby.
People come to cheer for their team.

Where in the World?

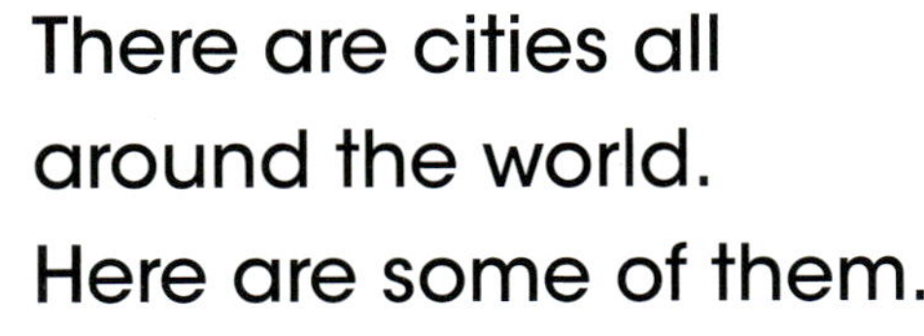

There are cities all around the world. Here are some of them.

New York in the United States has skyscrapers and theaters.

Rio de Janeiro in Brazil has mountains and beaches.

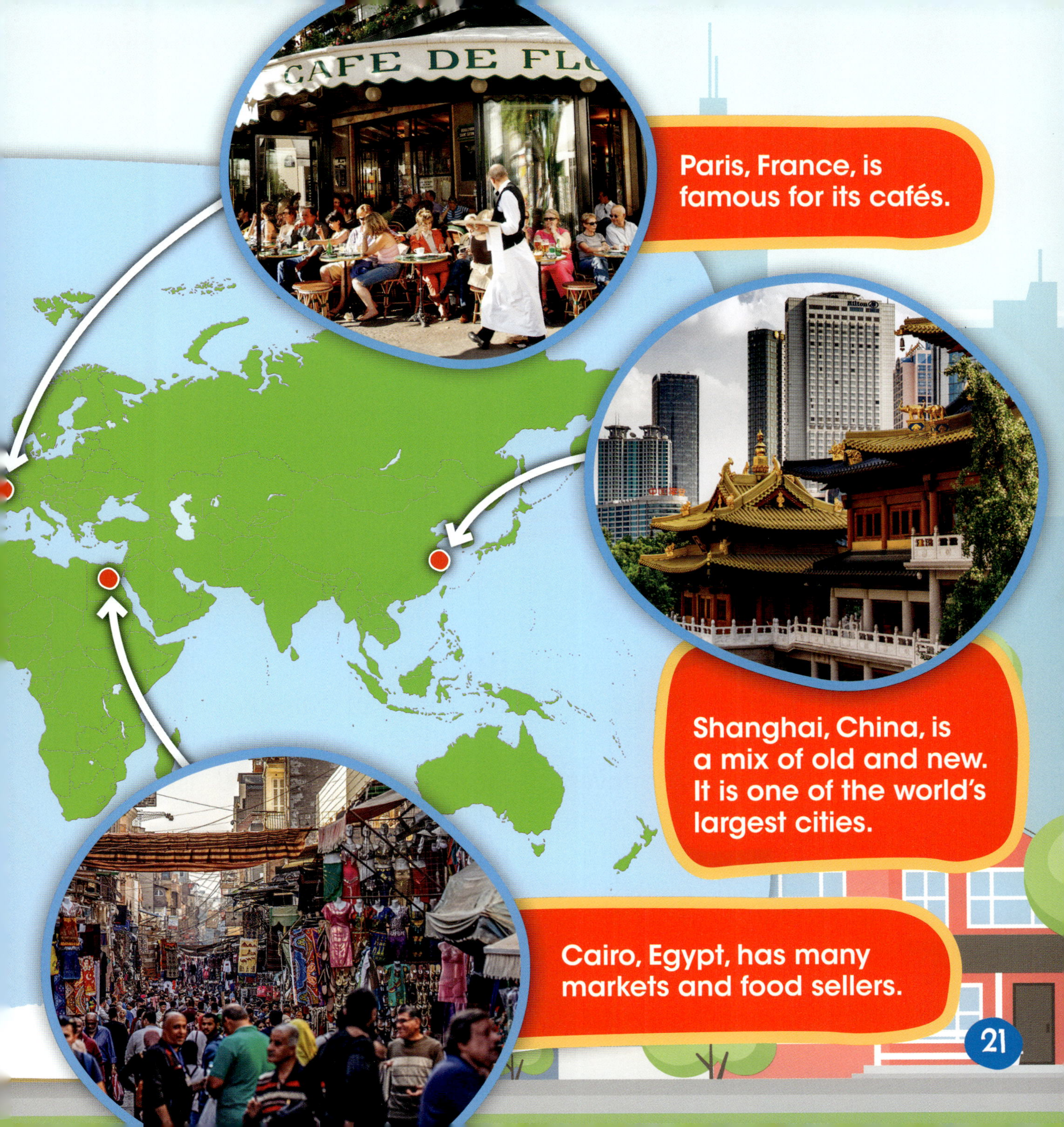

Paris, France, is famous for its cafés.

Shanghai, China, is a mix of old and new. It is one of the world's largest cities.

Cairo, Egypt, has many markets and food sellers.

Activities

Do you live in a city? If not, where is the nearest city? Find it on a map. Can you find out how many people live there?

Some people who live in tall apartment buildings use their balcony like a garden. What plants would you grow on your balcony? Plan a city garden.

Cities are full of people, but animals live there too. Choose a city animal such as a fox or pigeon and do research to learn more about how it survives.

Find Out More

Websites

kids.britannica.com/kids/article/city/352965

natgeokids.com/uk/discover/science/general-science/future-cities/

sciencefocus.com/planet-earth/in-pictures-the-largest-cities-in-the-world

Books

The Future of Cities Kevin Kurtz, Searchlight Books 2021

Skyscrapers Paige V. Polinsky, Sandcastle Books 2018

Up, Down, and Around the City Christianne Jones, Capstone 2022

Words to Know

apartment block a tall building divided up into many smaller apartments

balcony a platform that sticks out from the wall of a building, above the ground

canal a channel that is dug out to carry water, like an artificial river

crops plants that people grow to eat

deli a store that sells ready-to-eat food, such as salads or cooked meats

mayor an elected official who is in charge of a city

polluted dirty because of being contaminated with chemicals or waste

skyscraper a very tall building with many floors for apartments or offices

tourist a person who travels to a place on vacation to see the sights

townhouse a house that shares its side walls with the houses on each side of it

Index